Moshe's Adventures in Brachahland

Itamar Marcus

Illustrated by Liat Benyaminy Ariel

ALL RIGHTS RESERVED
©Copyright 1990, by MESORAH PUBLICATIONS, Ltd.
4401 Second Avenue / Brooklyn, N.Y. 11232 / (718) 921-9000
Produced by SEFERCRAFT, INC. / Brooklyn, N.Y.

One afternoon, Moshe came into the kitchen and found his mother preparing pizza. He saw all kinds of different foods on the counter: flour, tomato sauce, a chunk of hard cheese, and olives.

"I wonder what *brachah* I say before eating pizza," he said. "There are so many foods in pizza and each one has a different *brachah.*"

"That's a terrific question," his mother replied. "And as soon as I've finished preparing this pizza I'll be happy to answer your question."

Moshe decided to go upstairs and wait in his room. But, as he opened the door to the room, a strange thing happened. From the window, behind the curtain, he heard a mysterious voice.

"Your mother is very busy right now," said the voice, "and that's why she could not answer your question right away."

Moshe stared at the window. Then, slowly, he walked towards the voice. Carefully, he moved the curtain aside. There, standing in his window, was a giant pizza.

"Please excuse me for dropping in like this without an invitation," said the surprising visitor. "I hope I'm not disturbing you, but I think I can answer your question."

"N-not at all," answered a confused Moshe. "But who are you?"

"I am the Magical Shaltiel. Magical — because like magic I can change into anything I please. And Shaltiel (which comes from the Hebrew word for question) — because I love to answer questions about Torah and *mitzvos.*"

Moshe stared at the odd but friendly stranger. He was so excited he couldn't think of anything to say.

"To answer your question, I have changed myself into a flying pizza," Shaltiel continued. "Will you join me for a trip to Brachahland?"

"Brachahland?" Moshe asked. "What's that?"

"It's a wonderful place where farmers grow all the foods that we eat," answered Shaltiel. "Are you ready?"

"Sure!" answered Moshe. "But please remember, I have to be back home soon."

Moshe climbed onto Shaltiel's crust and out the window they flew. High up into the clouds they soared, away from the city and out into the country.

"What are you when you're not a pizza?" Moshe asked.

"When I'm not a pizza I . . . oh, look over there," he called out excitedly, without finishing his answer. "We are very close to Brachahland."

Moshe stared ahead at the beautiful sight. The earth was a checkerboard of colored fields which seemed to

"Wow!" Moshe exclaimed. "There's so much to remember! My head is beginning to spin like a Chanukah *dreidel.*"

"Don't get tired now," said Shaltiel. "There's still more to see and learn. Lots more. Are you ready?"

"Let's go!" said Moshe, and off they flew.

"Now we'll learn about cheese," explained Shaltiel, as they landed in an animal farm. "Many baby animals are not able to find food for themselves, so *Hashem* made certain that they would be taken care of. Some animals drink milk that comes from their mothers."

"Cow's milk is good for calves, but people drink it as well, and it can be made into cheese for pizza. The *brachah* for milk, as well as other foods like honey or meat that don't grow from the ground, is *Shehakol*."

Moshe walked over to a small calf and patted her head.

"Isn't that funny," he said to the calf. "You and I drink the same milk! Thank you for sharing with me."

Moshe picked up some hay and fed the animals. Then he raced back to Shaltiel, leaped into the air, and landed with a plop on his flying friend.

"Ouch," he said. "Take it easy! I'm a flying pizza, not a trampoline!"

"I'm sorry," Moshe said. "I hope I didn't hurt you."

"I think I'm all right," said Shaltiel, as he checked his dough for holes and spread out his tomato sauce. Finally, they took off for another field.